Lazy Dog

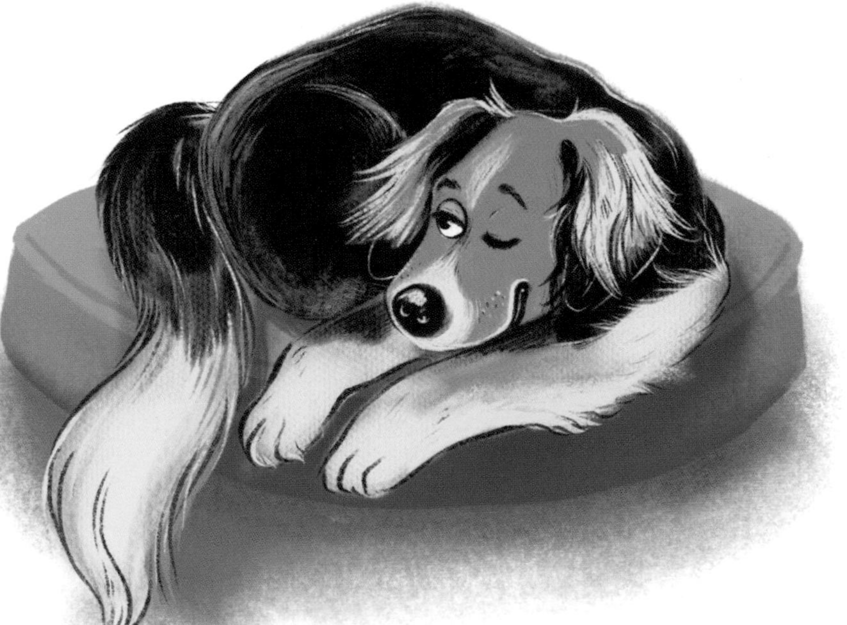

Story by
Gemma McMullen

Illustrated by
Angelika Waigand

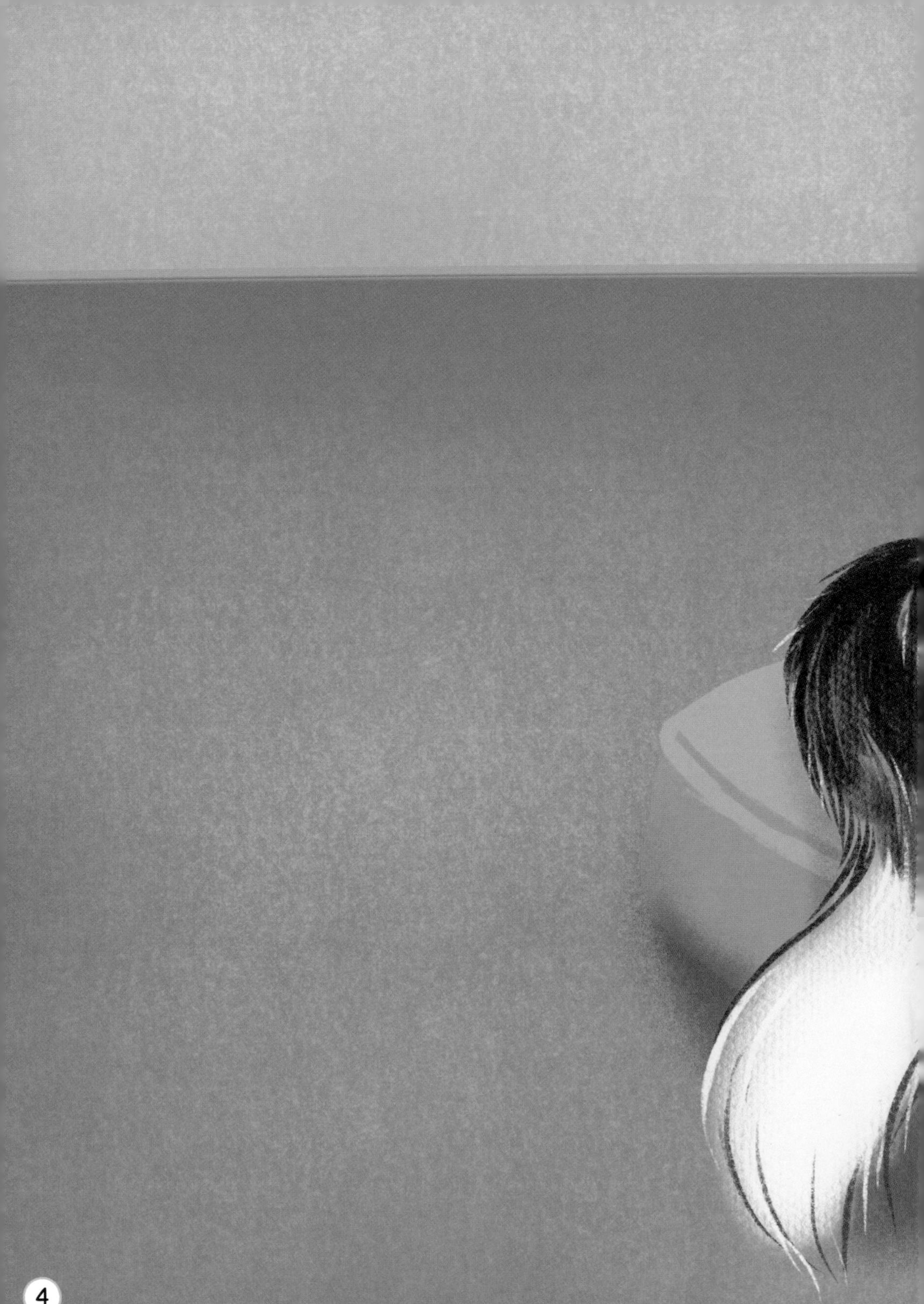

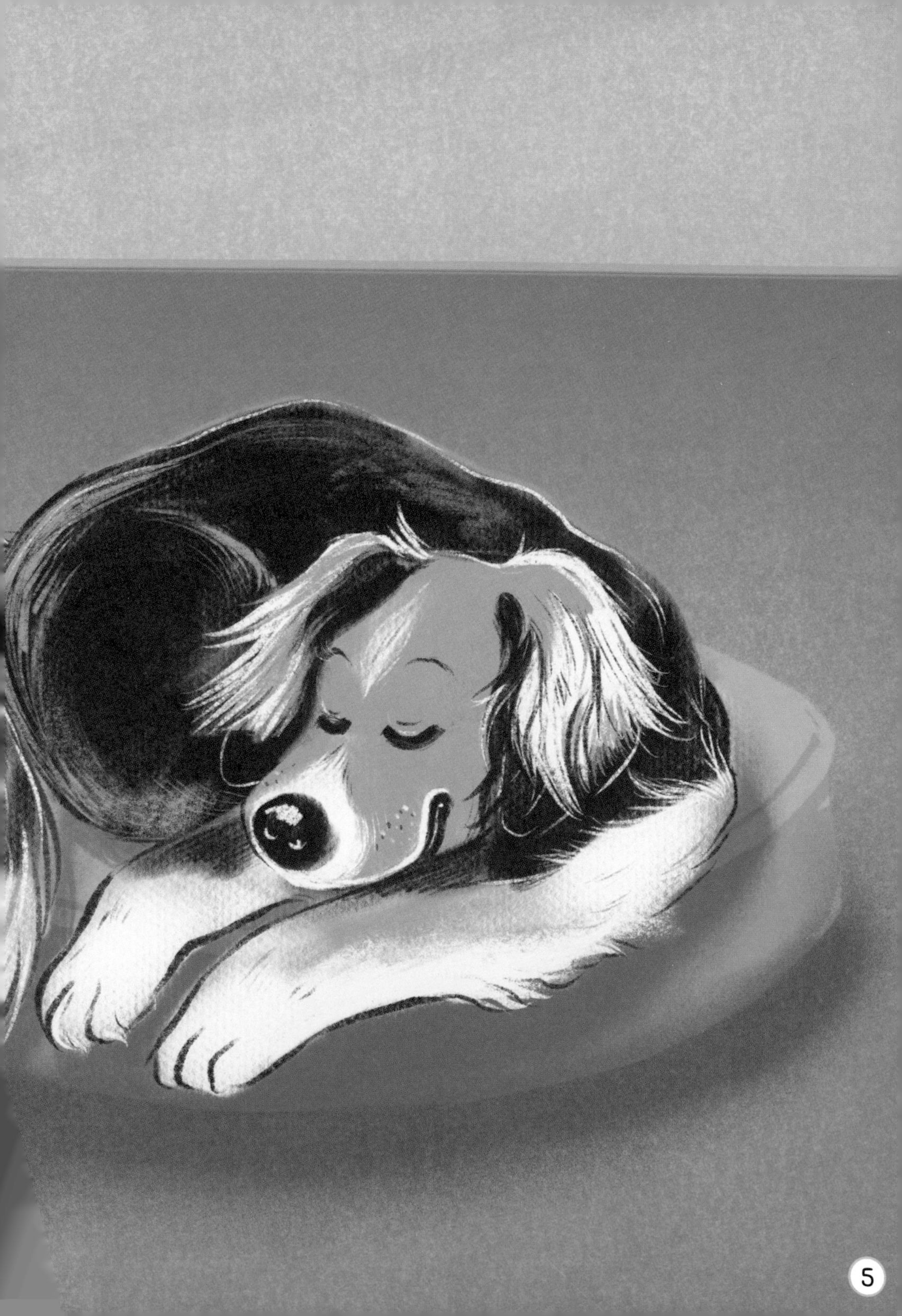

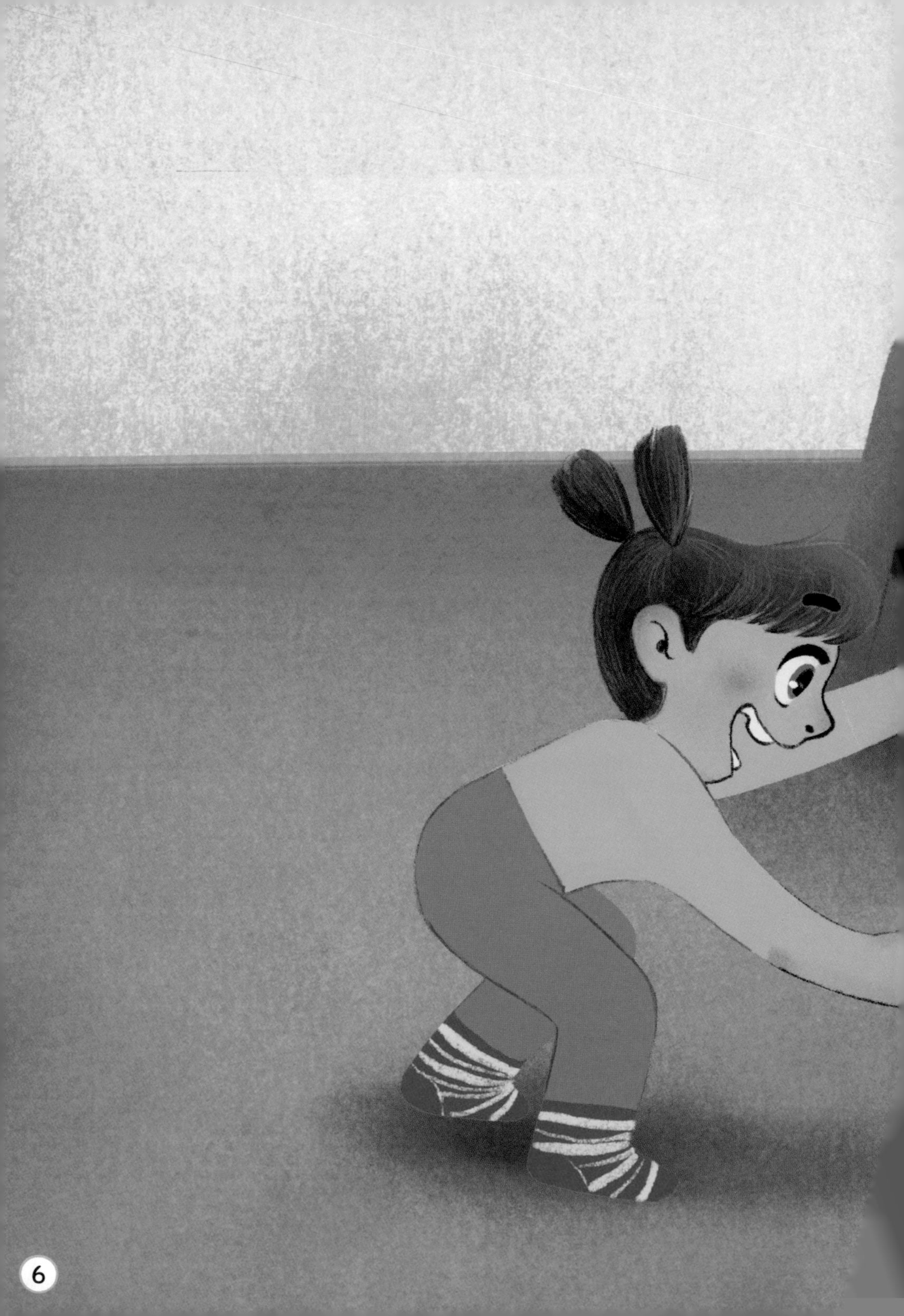

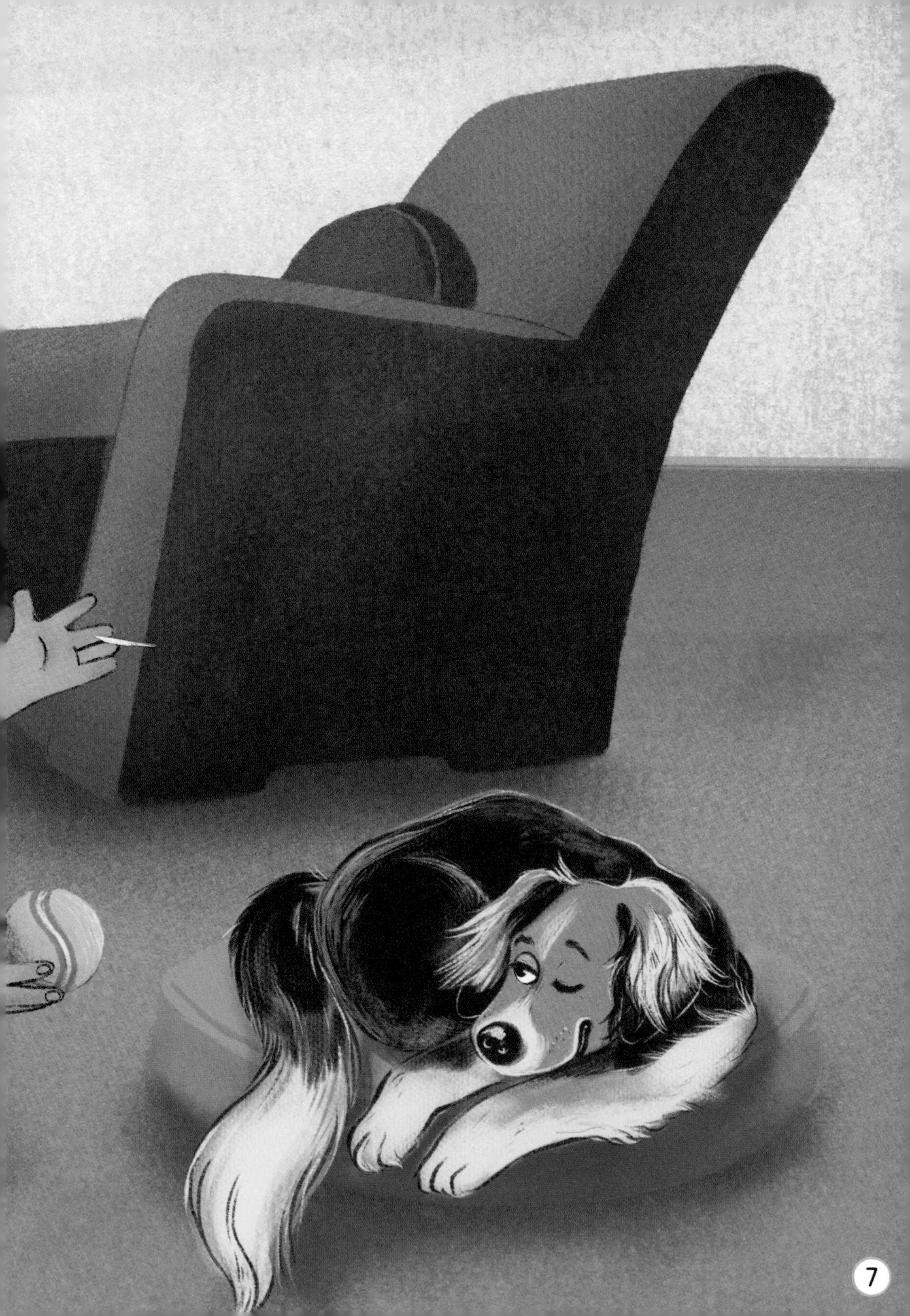

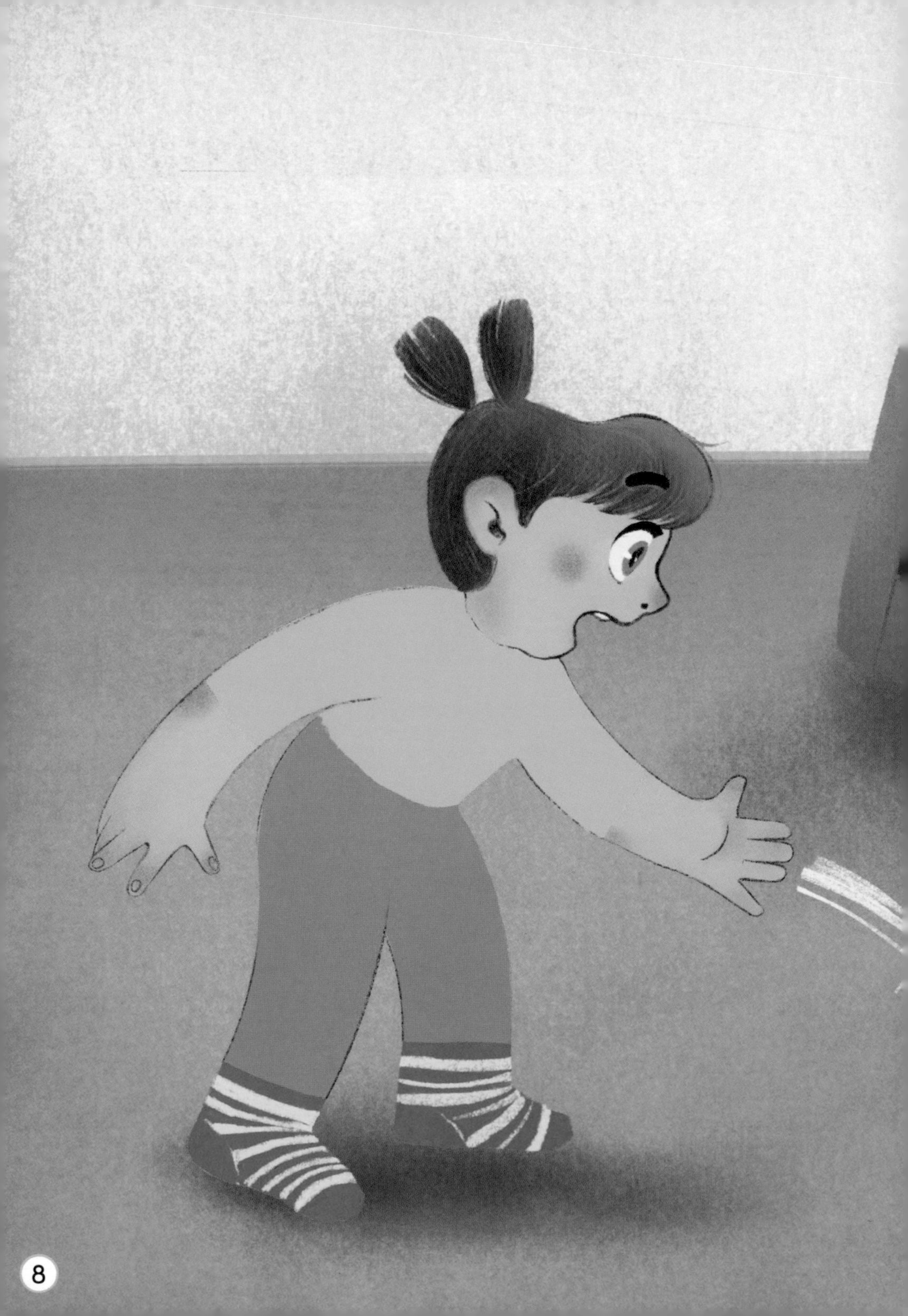

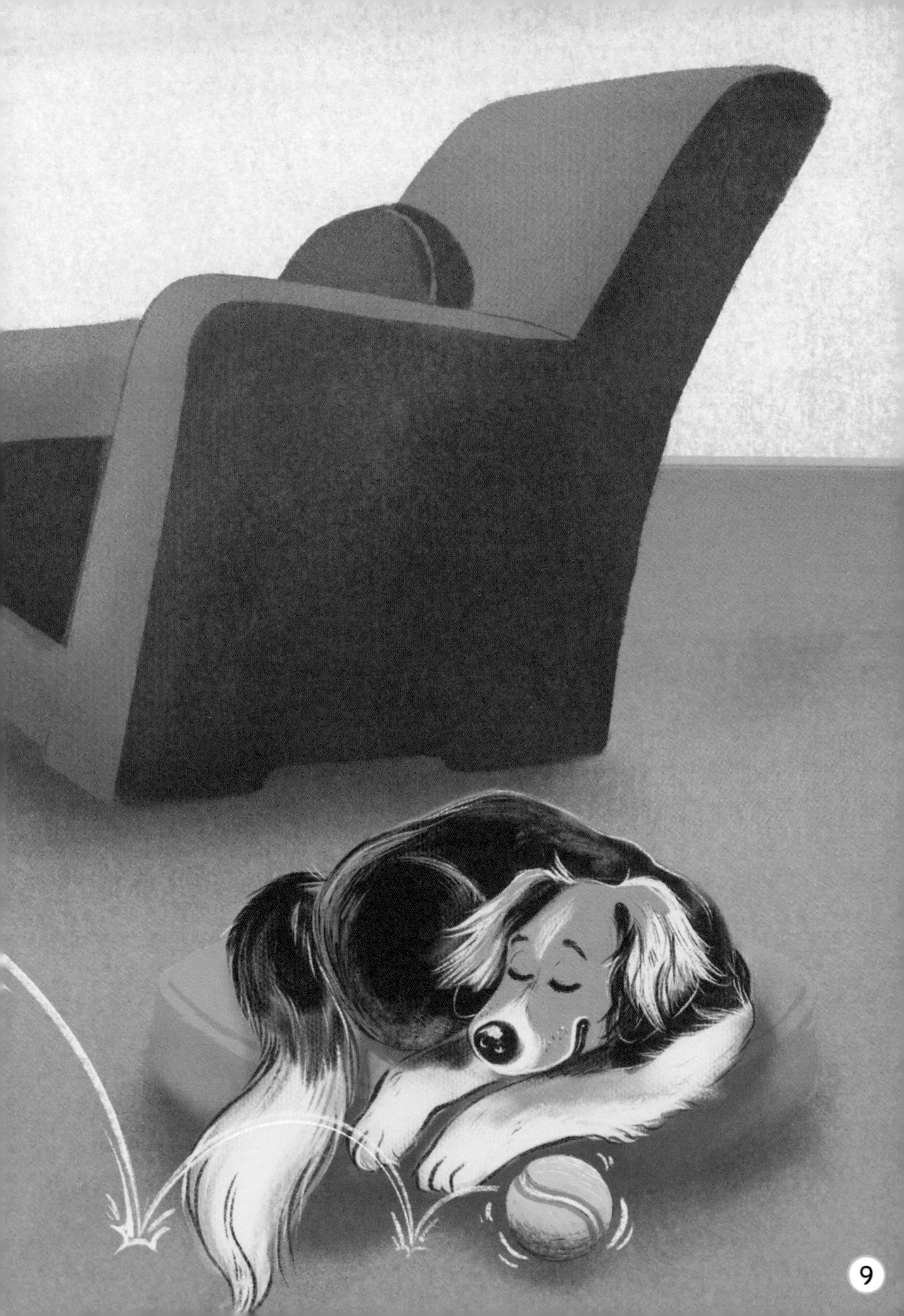

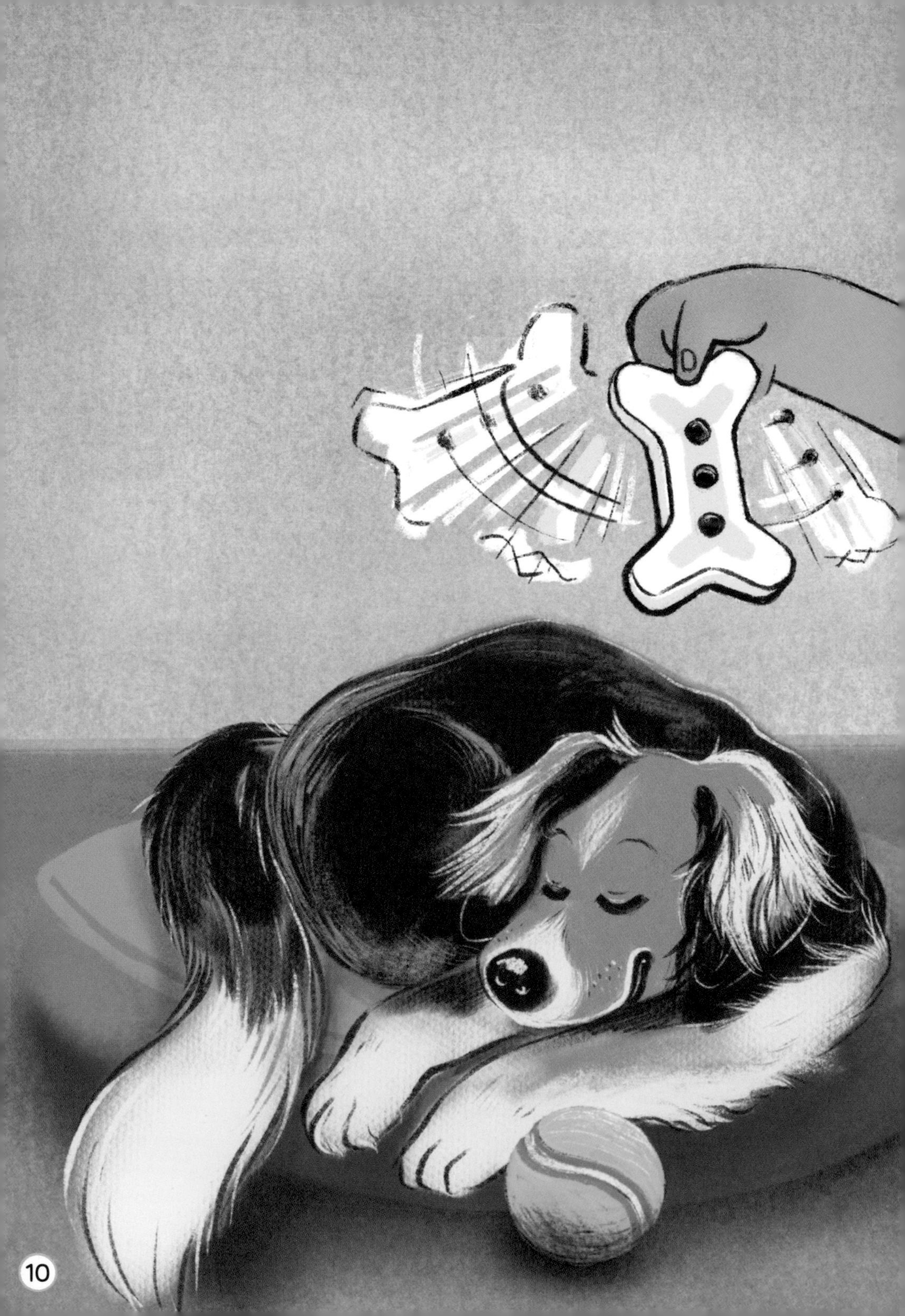

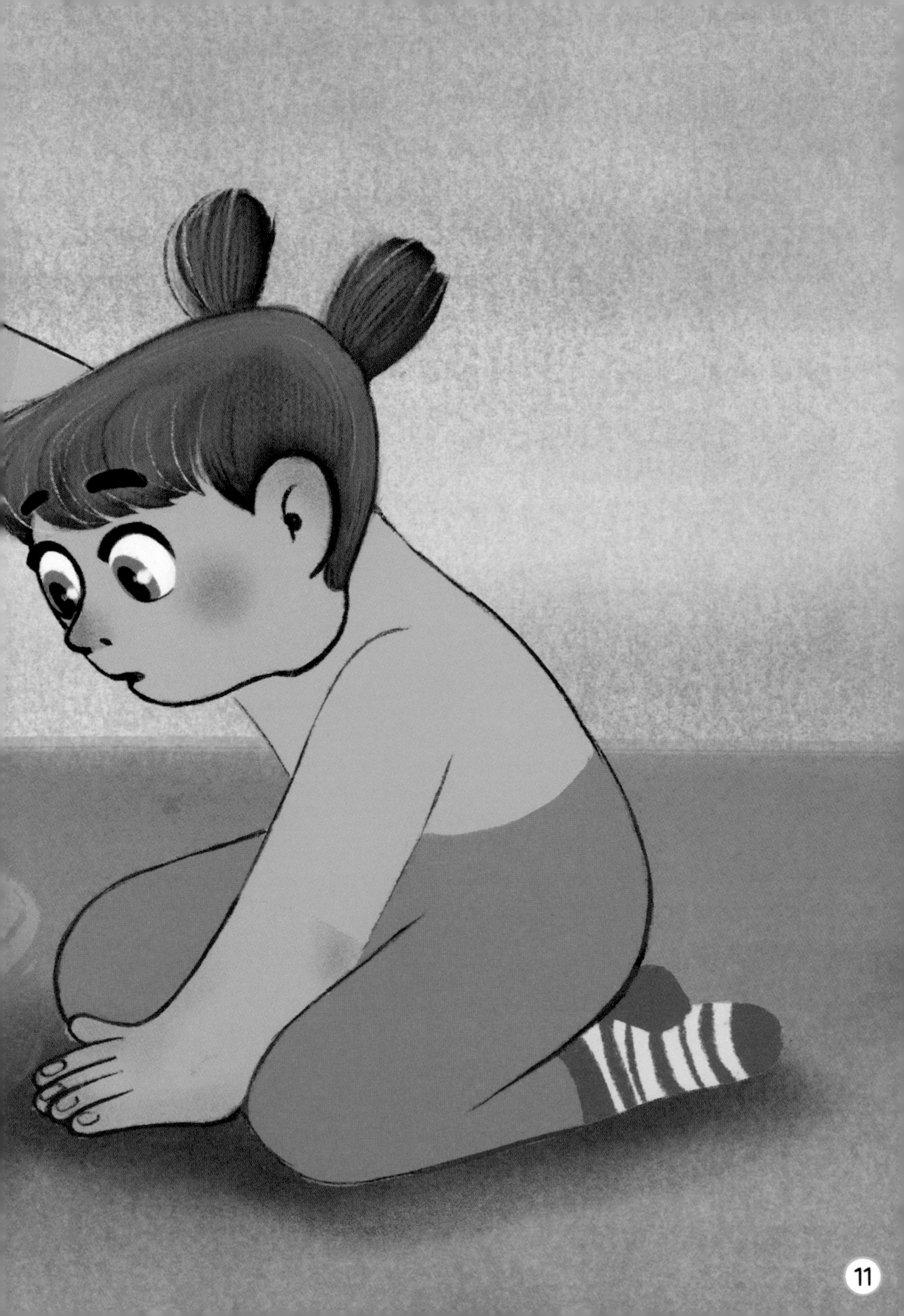

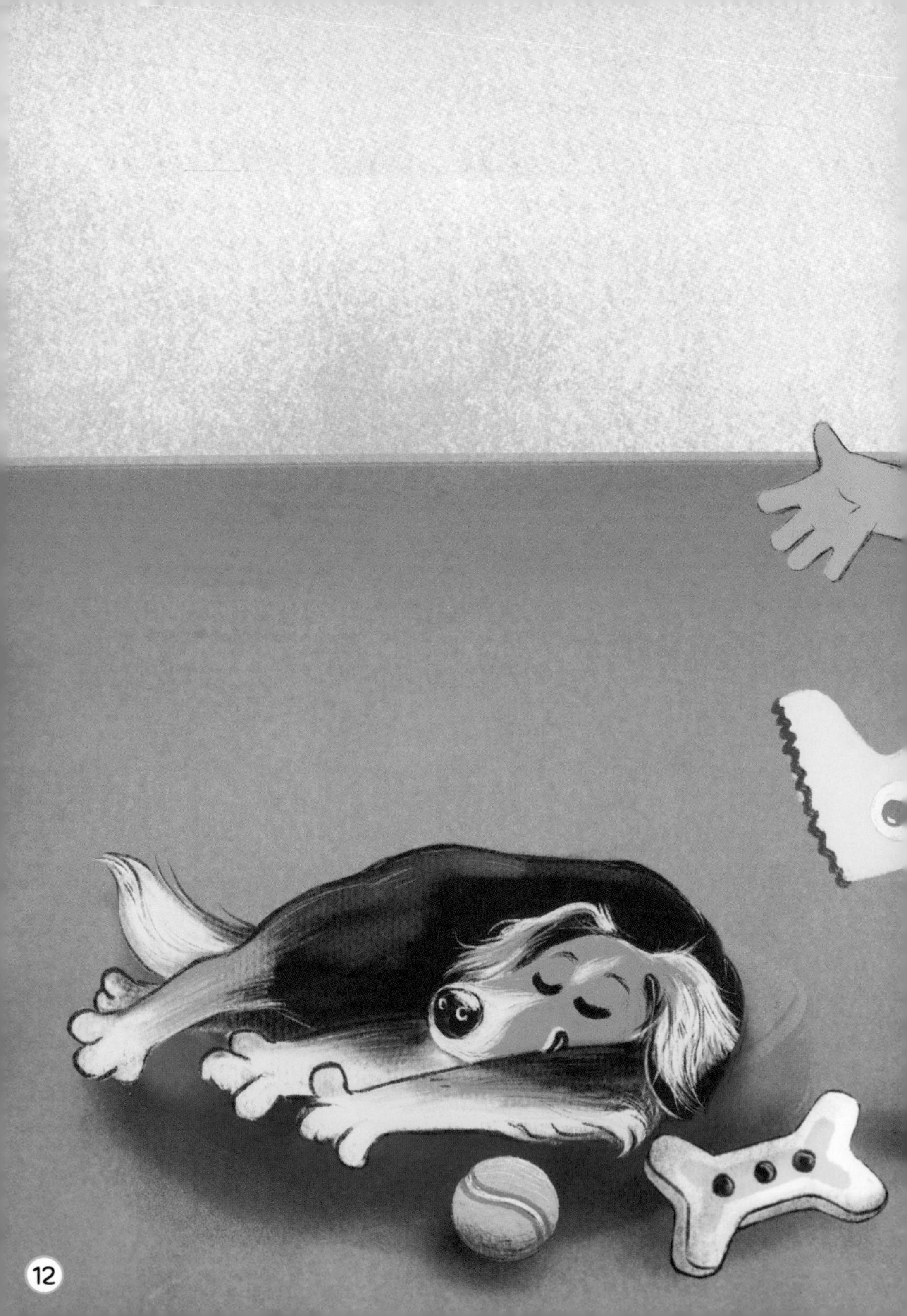

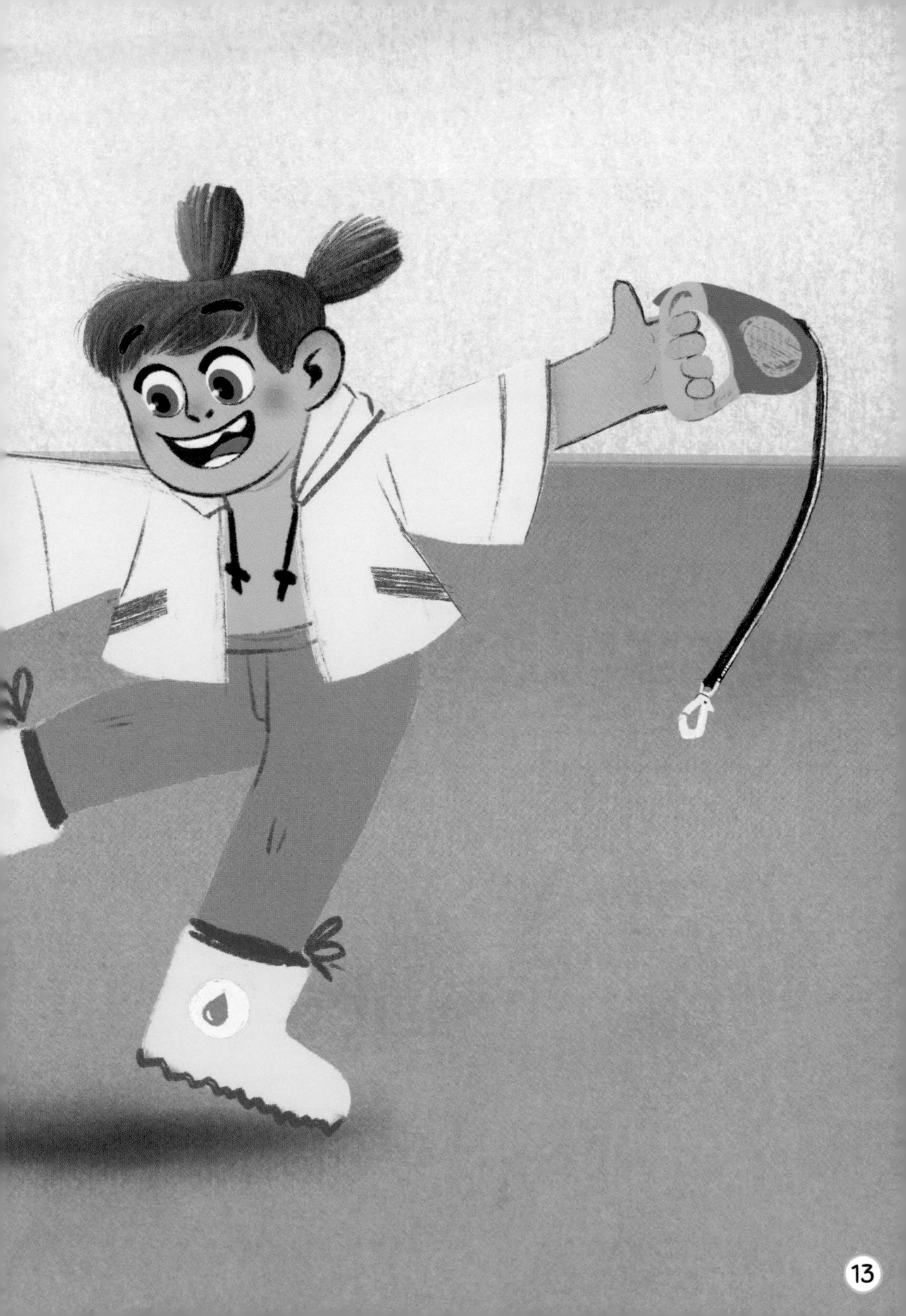

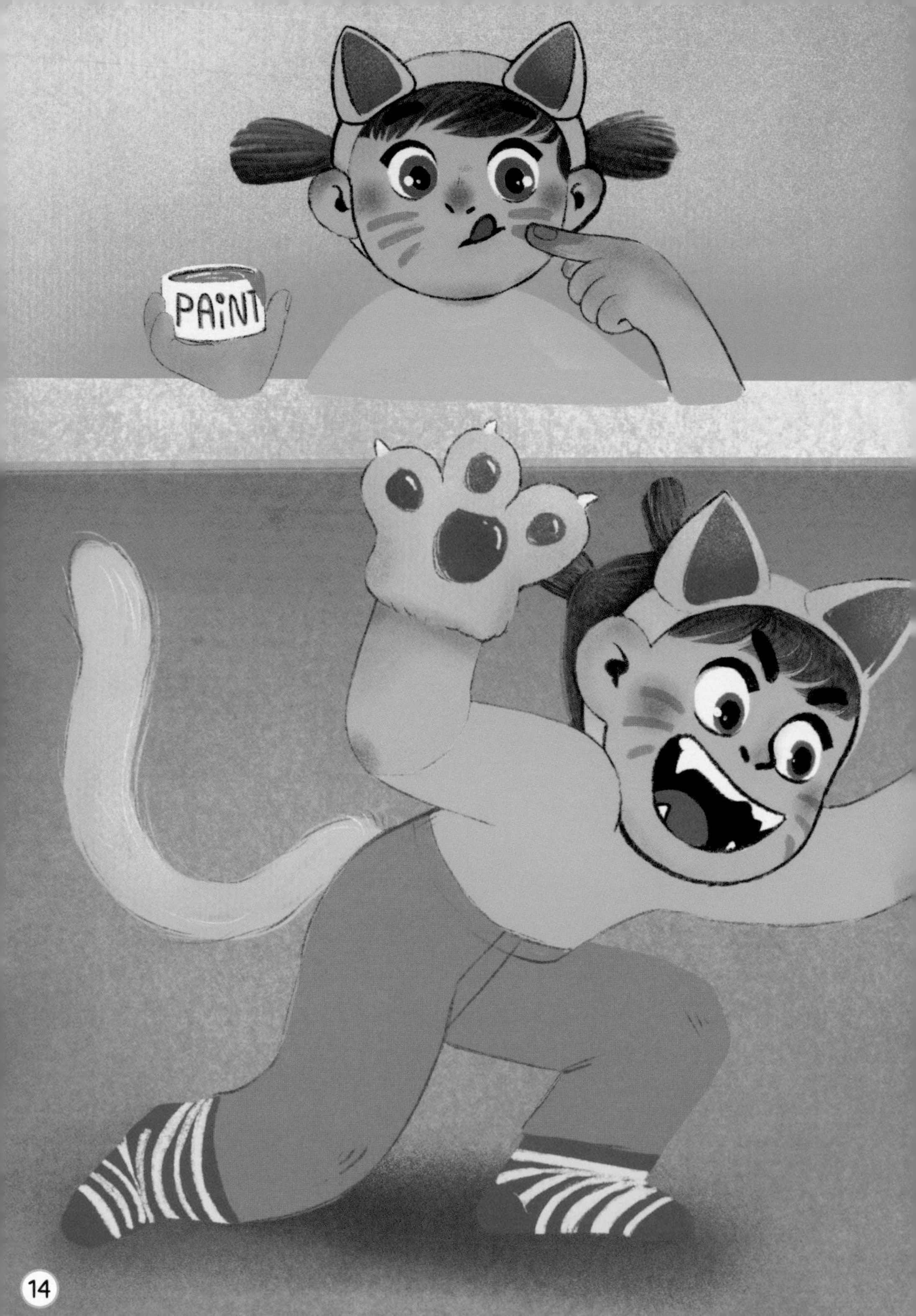
PAiNT

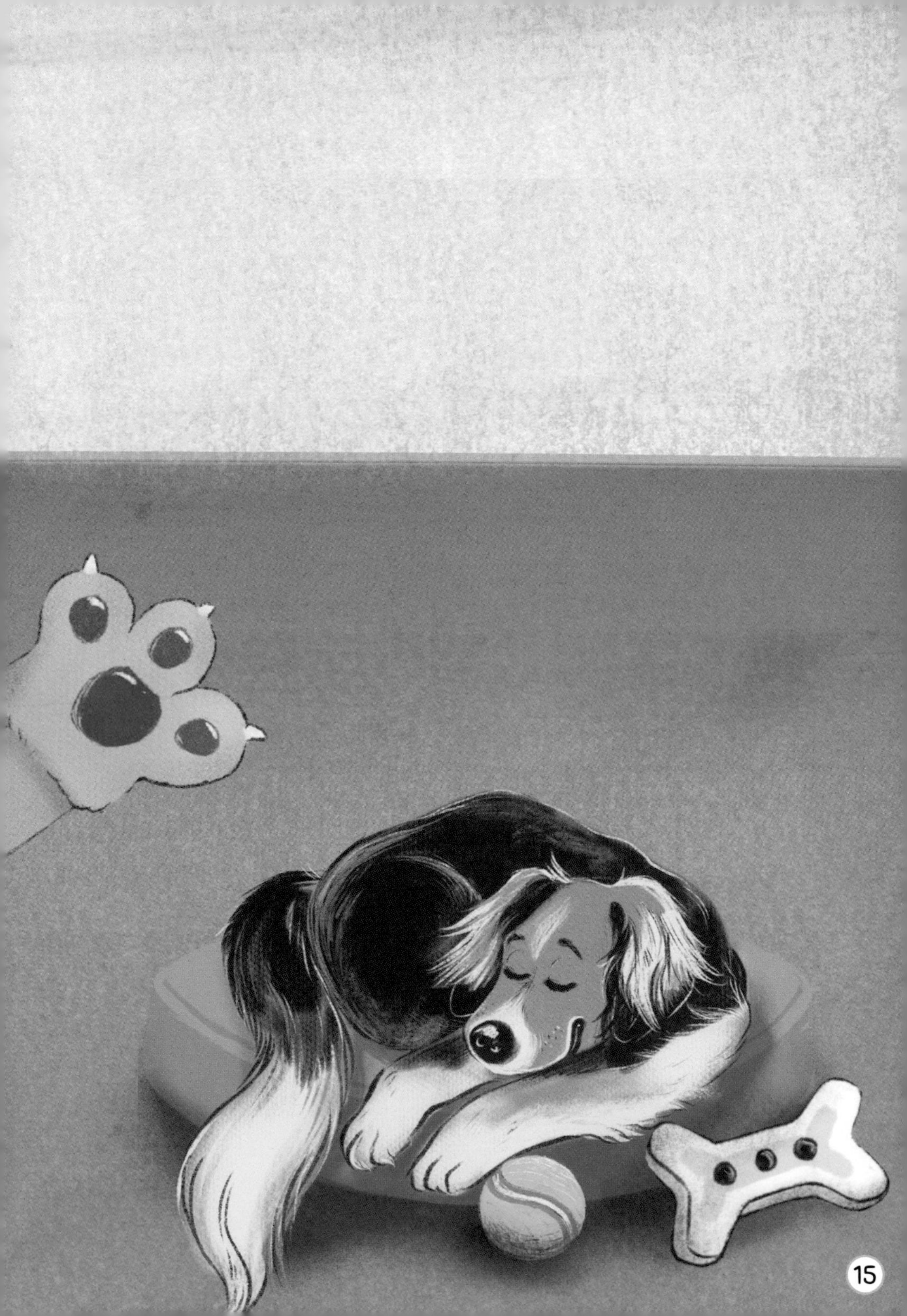

Panic at the Beach

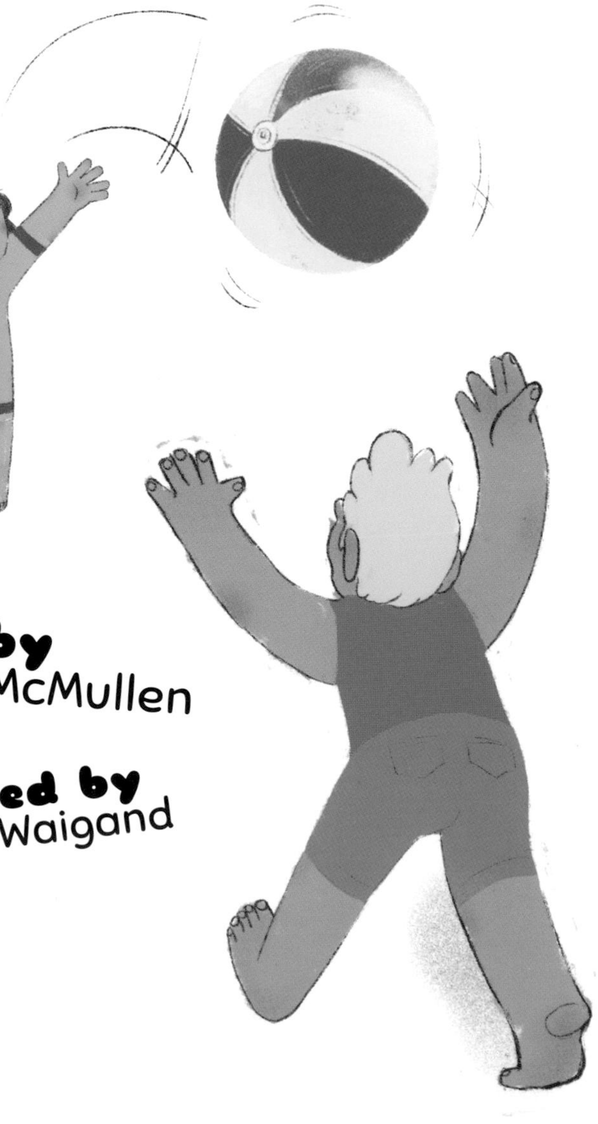

Story by
Gemma McMullen

Illustrated by
Angelika Waigand

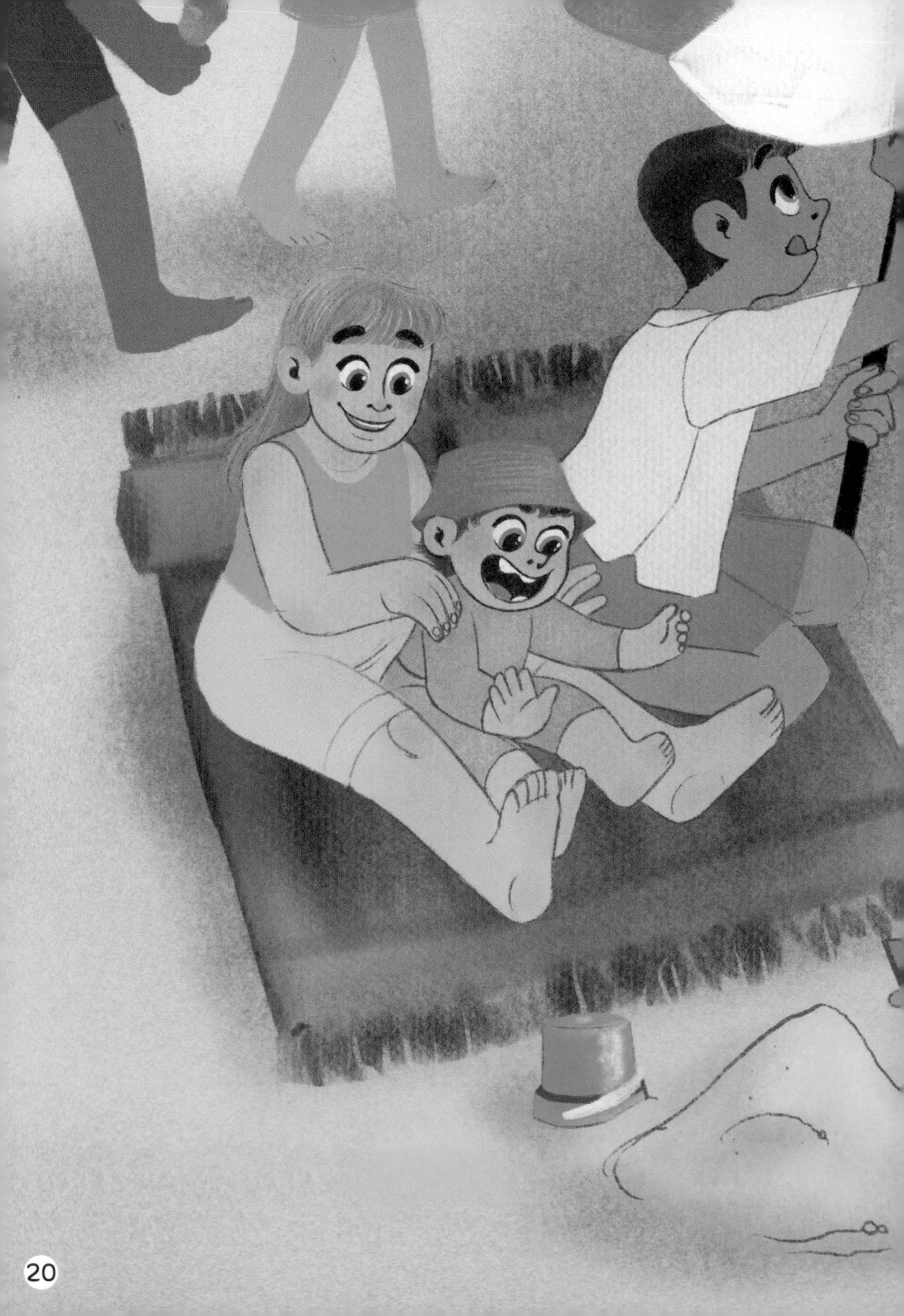

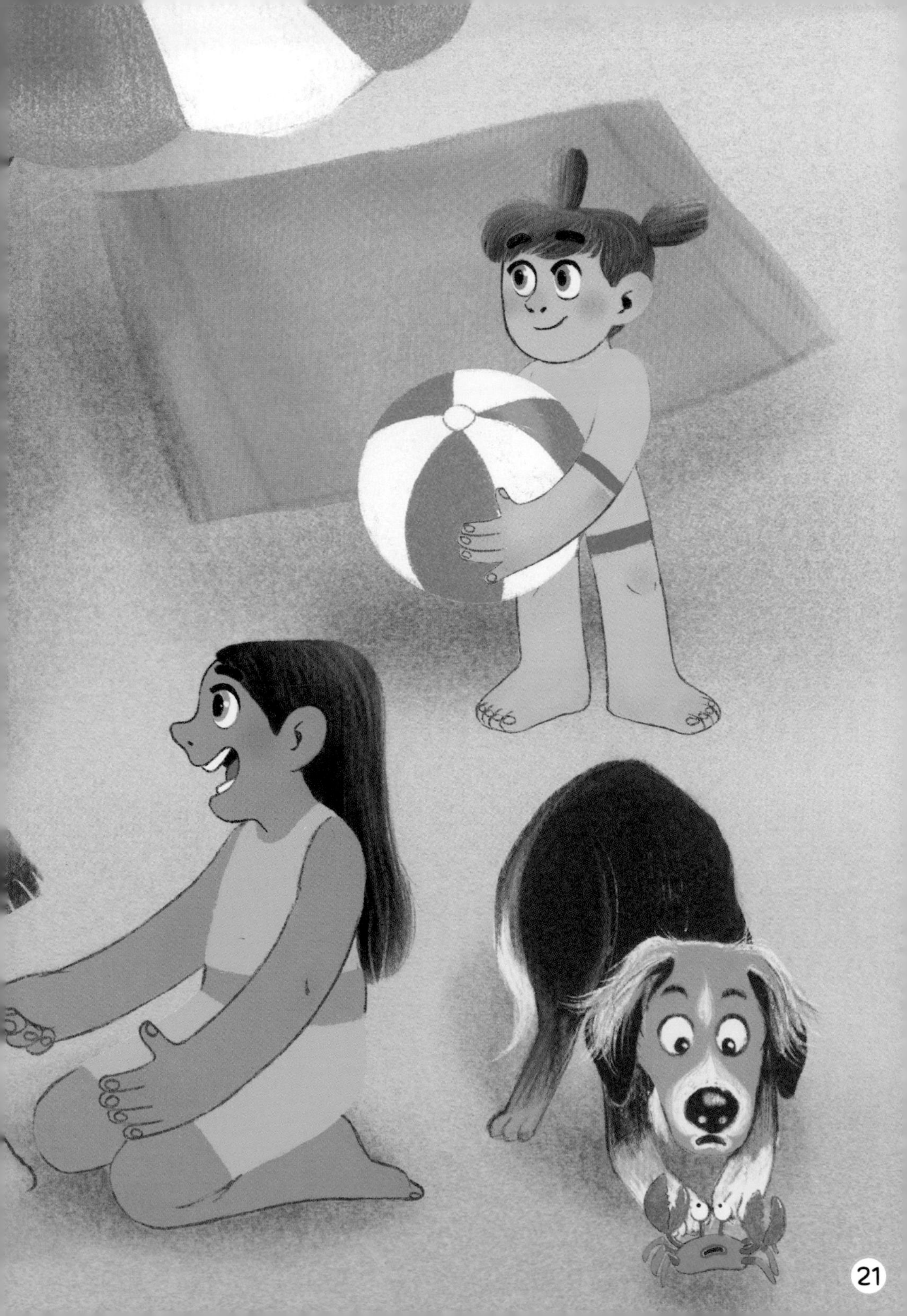

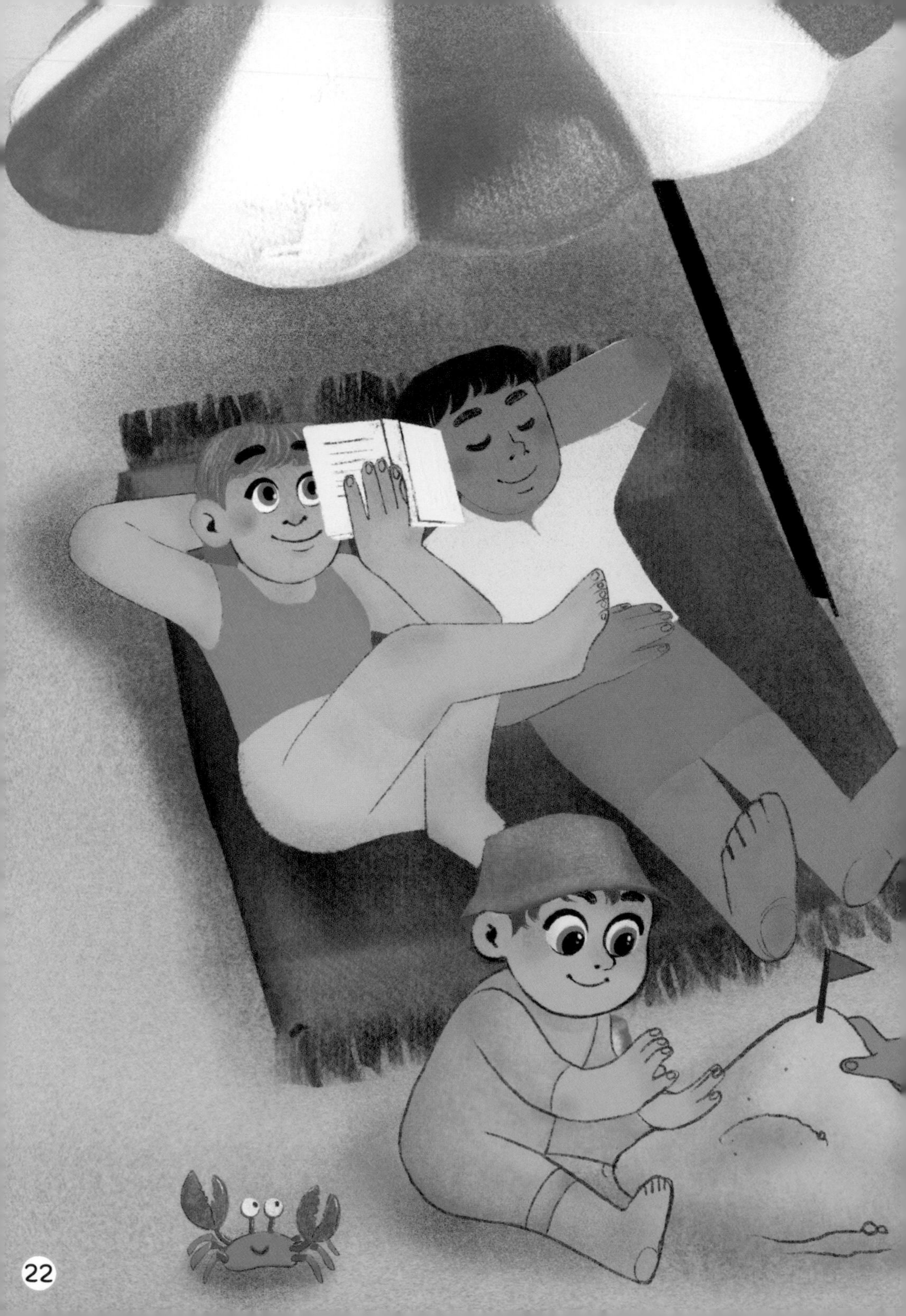

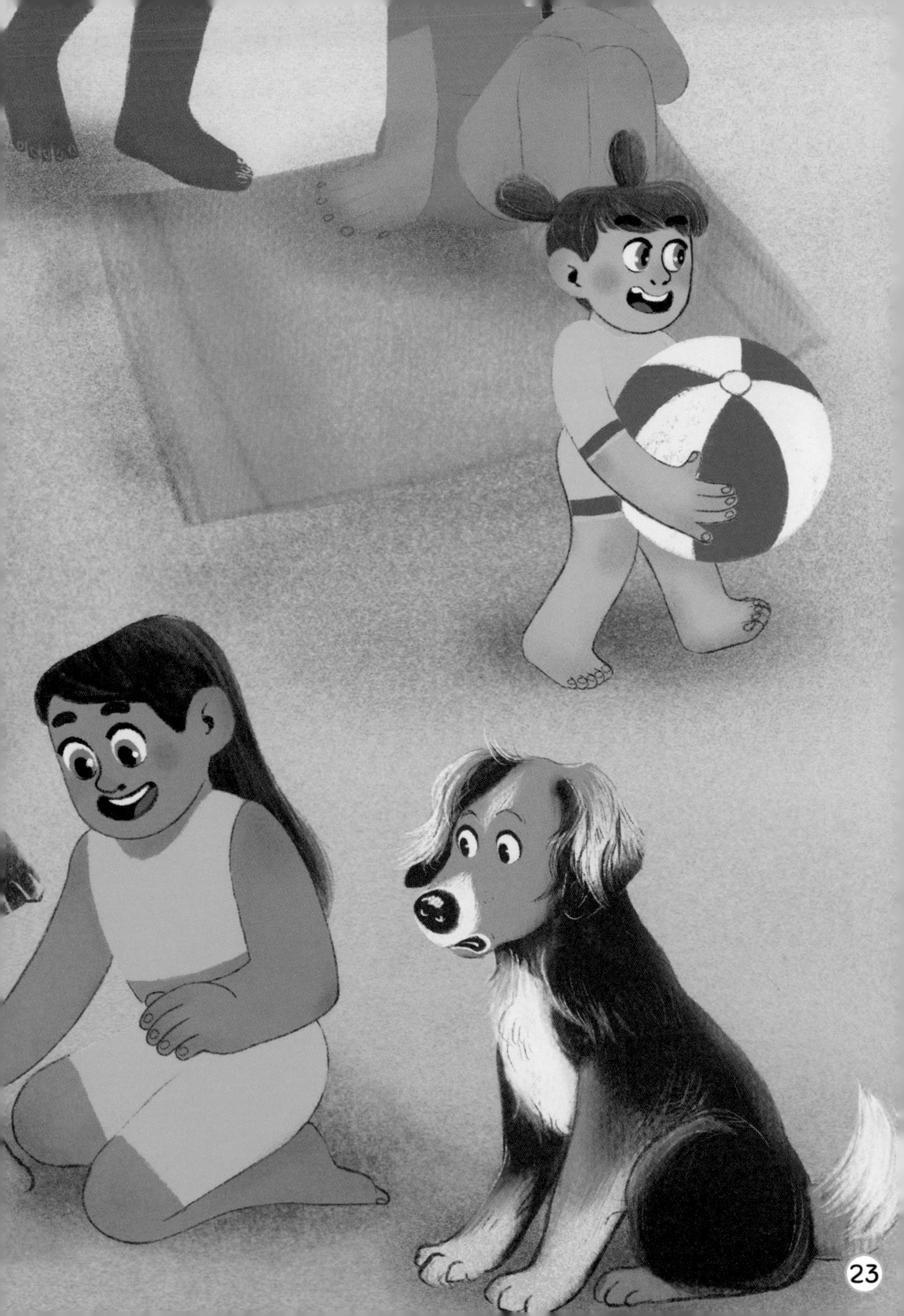

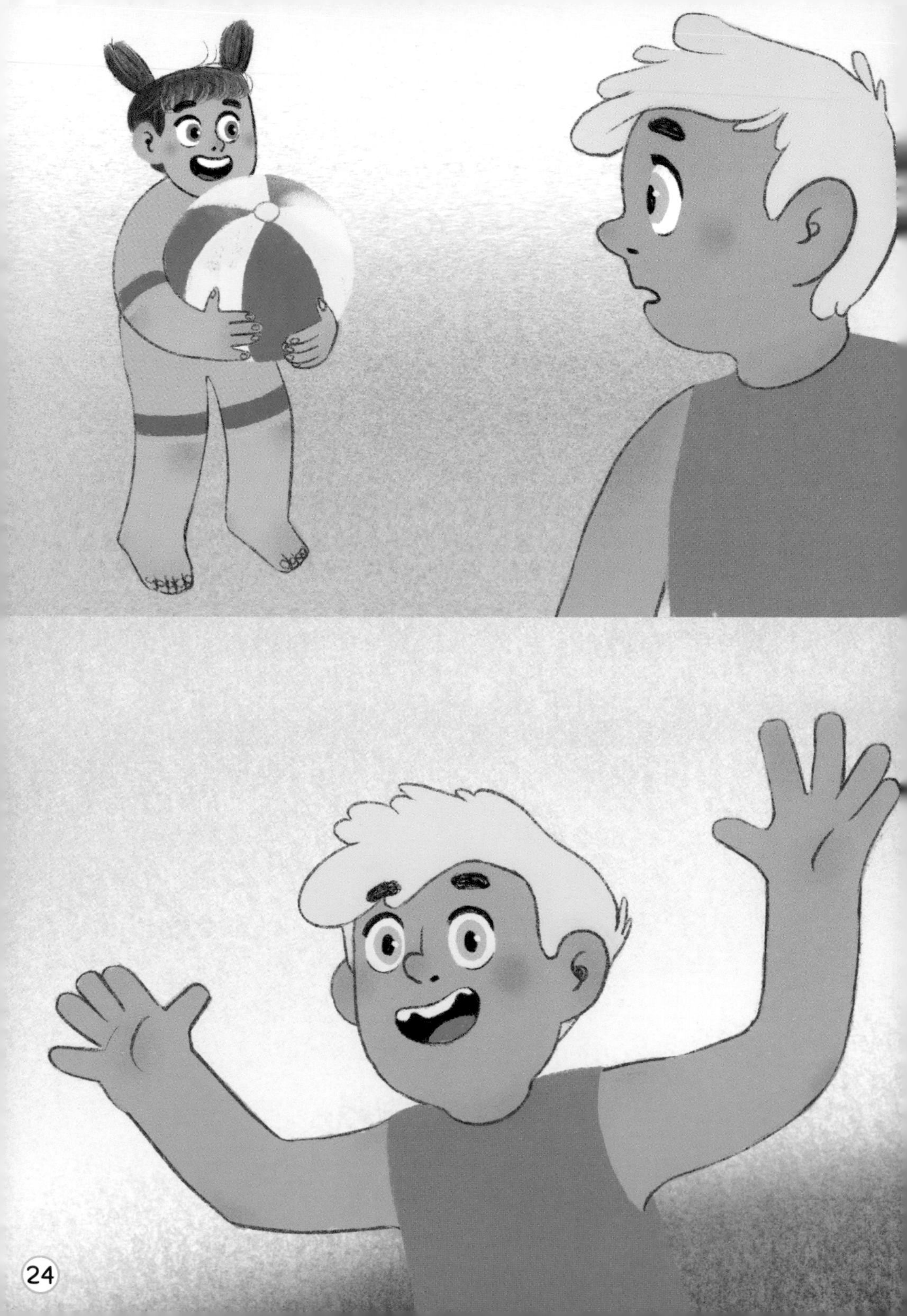

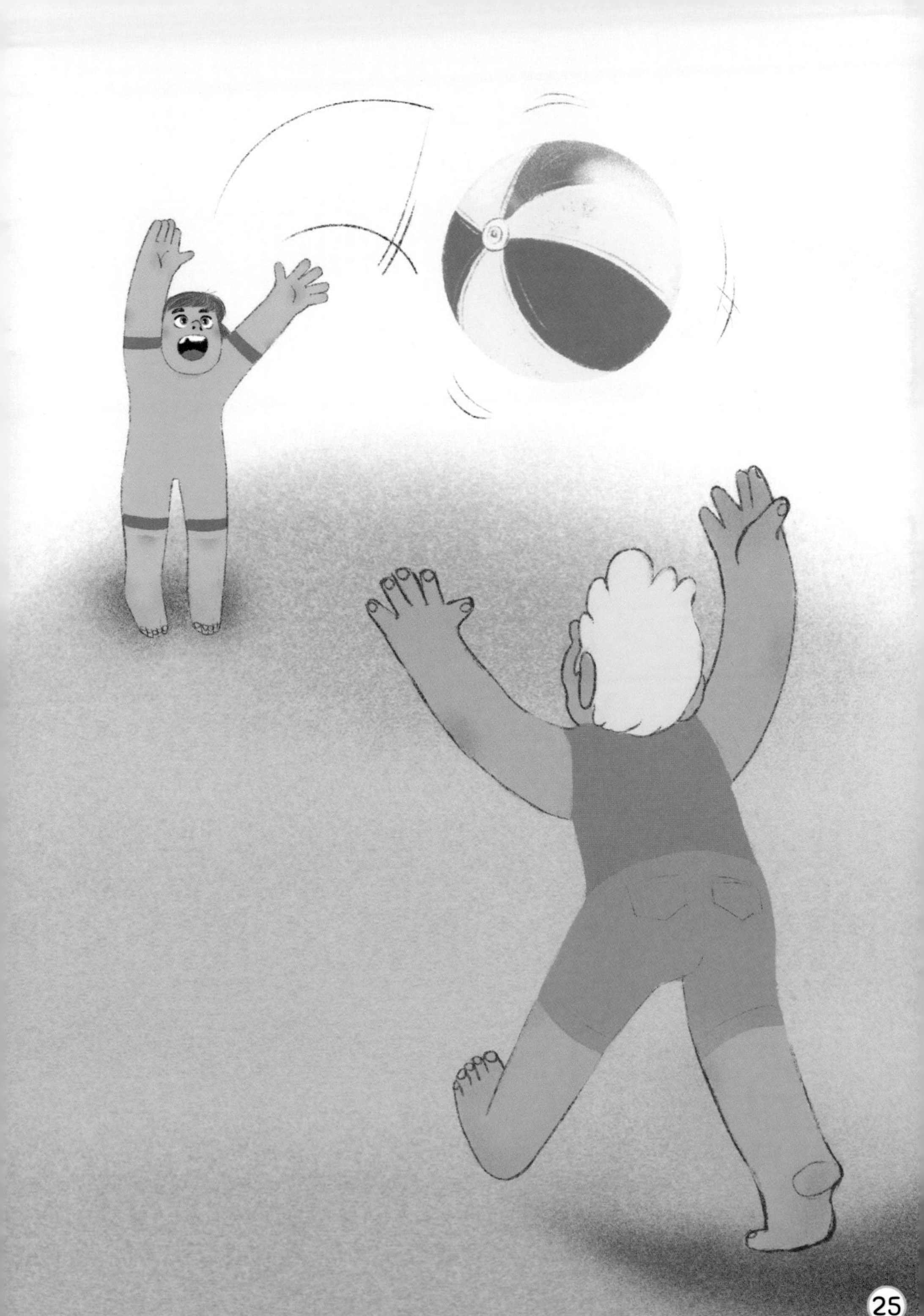

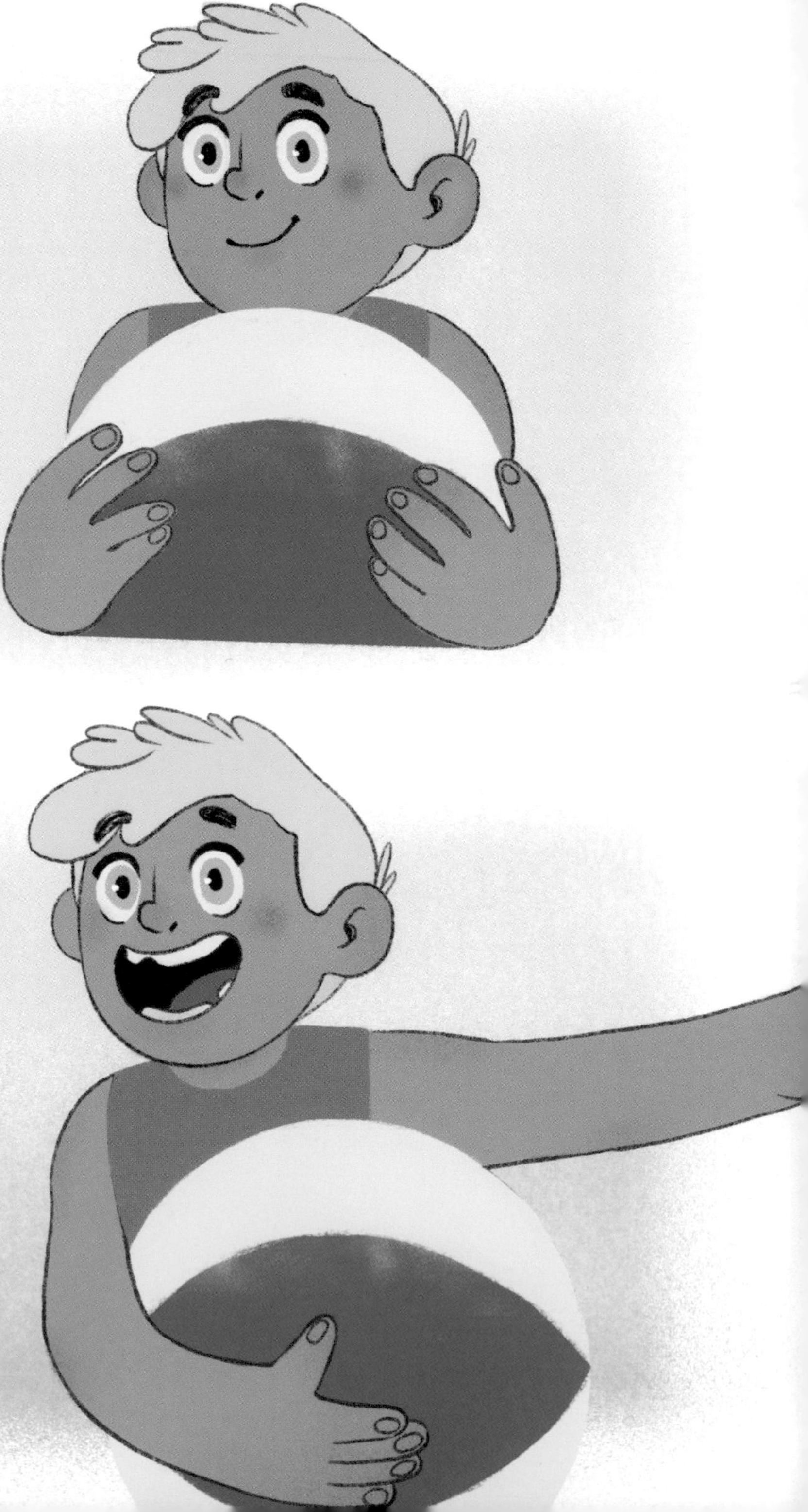

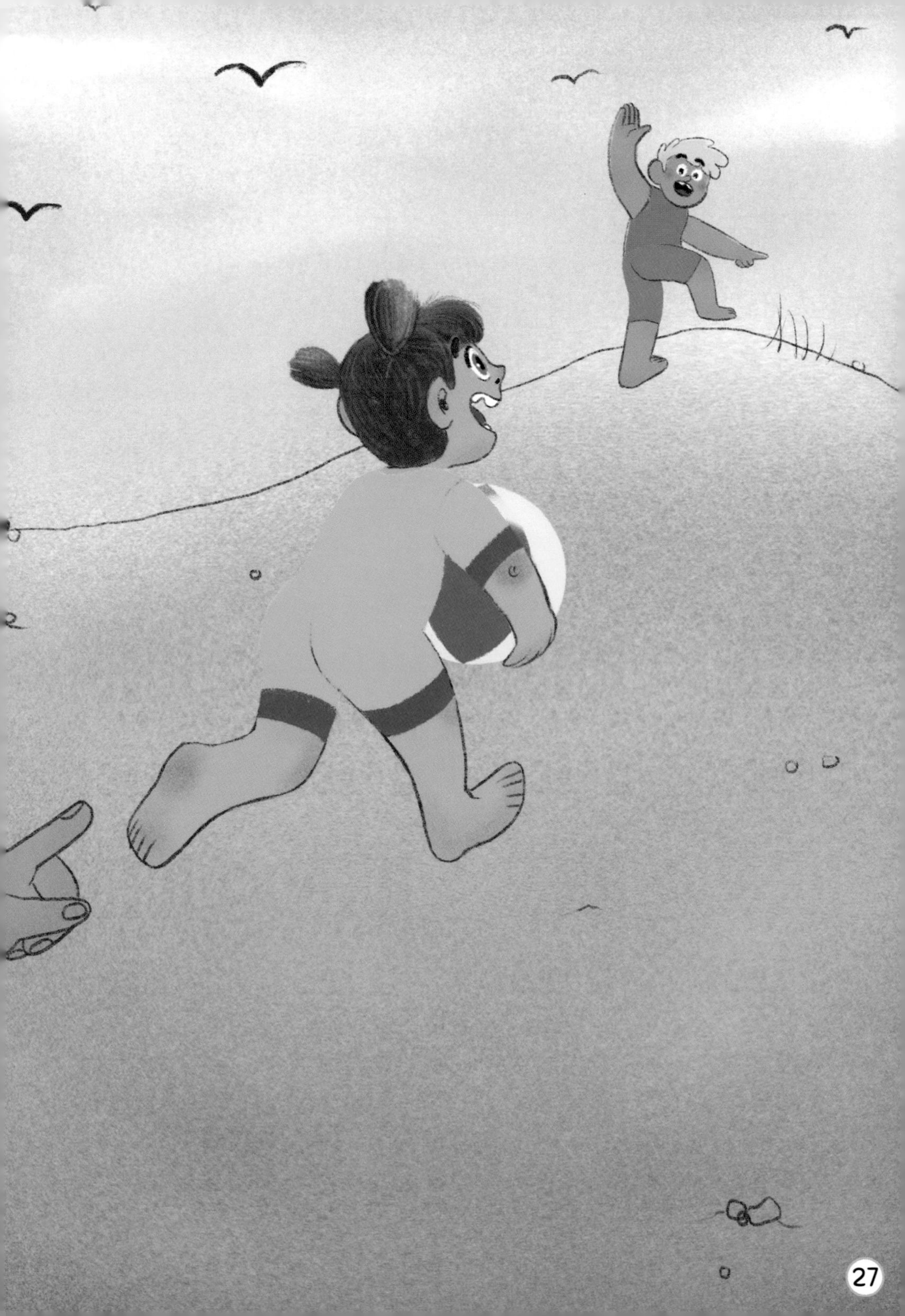

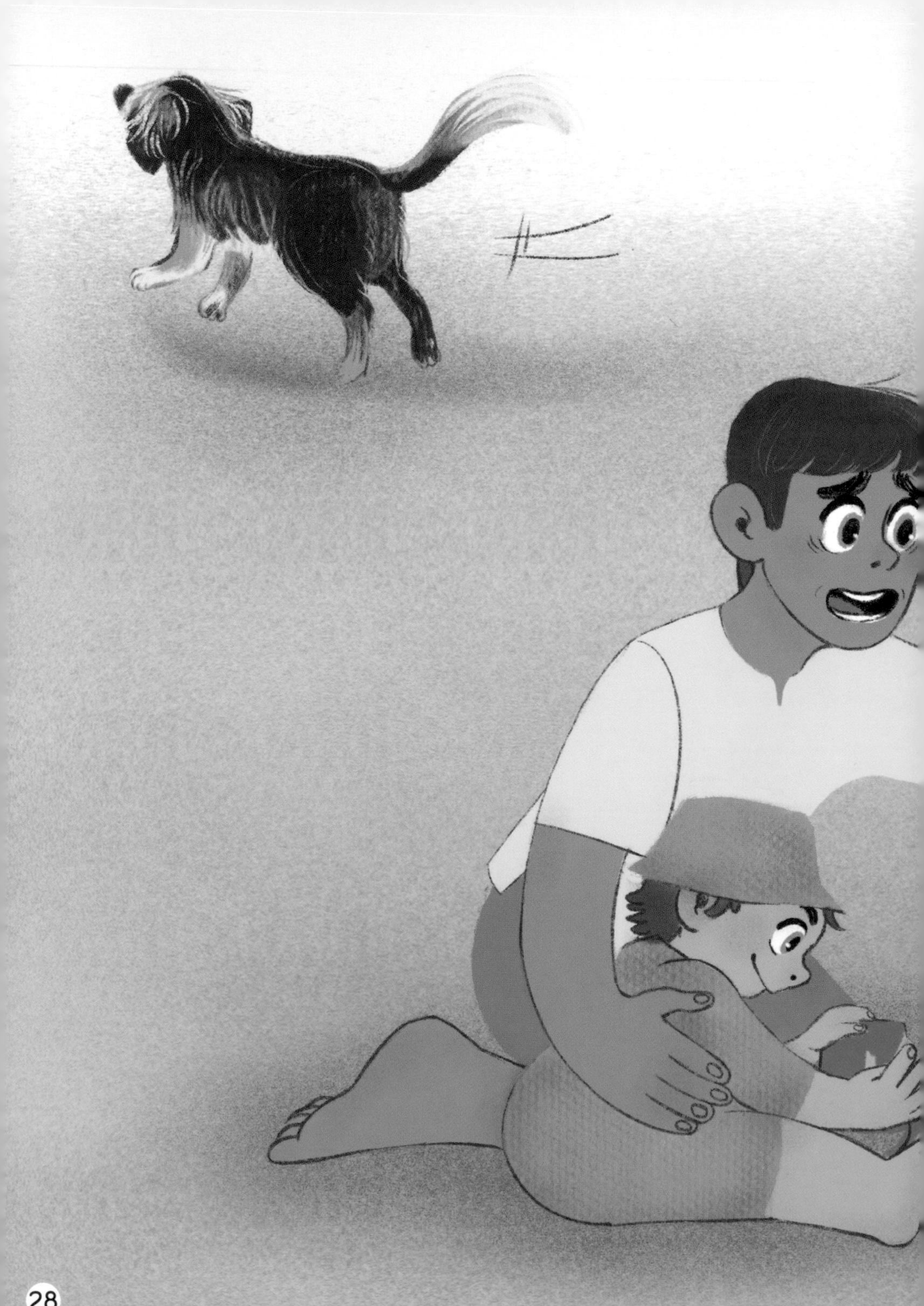

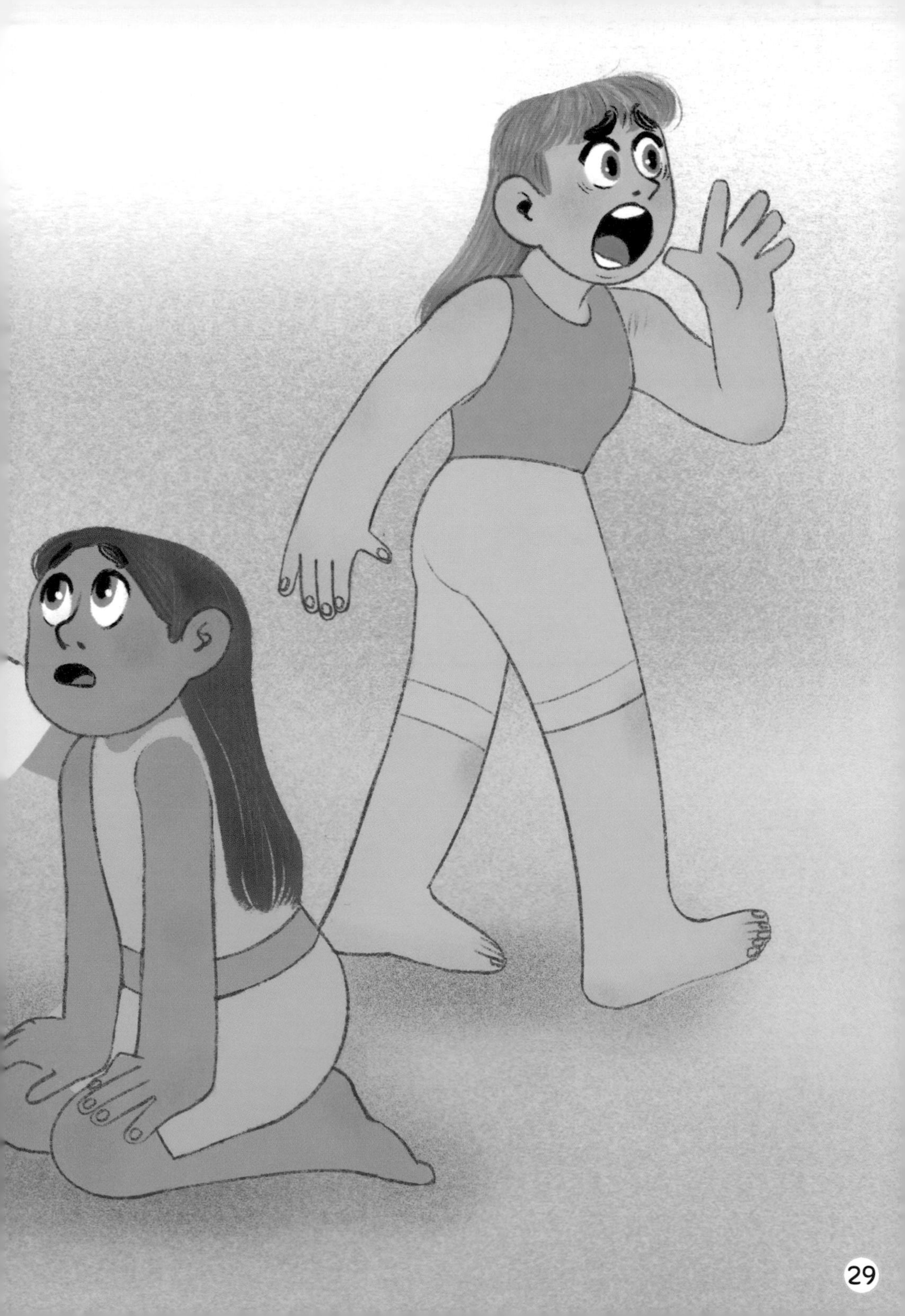

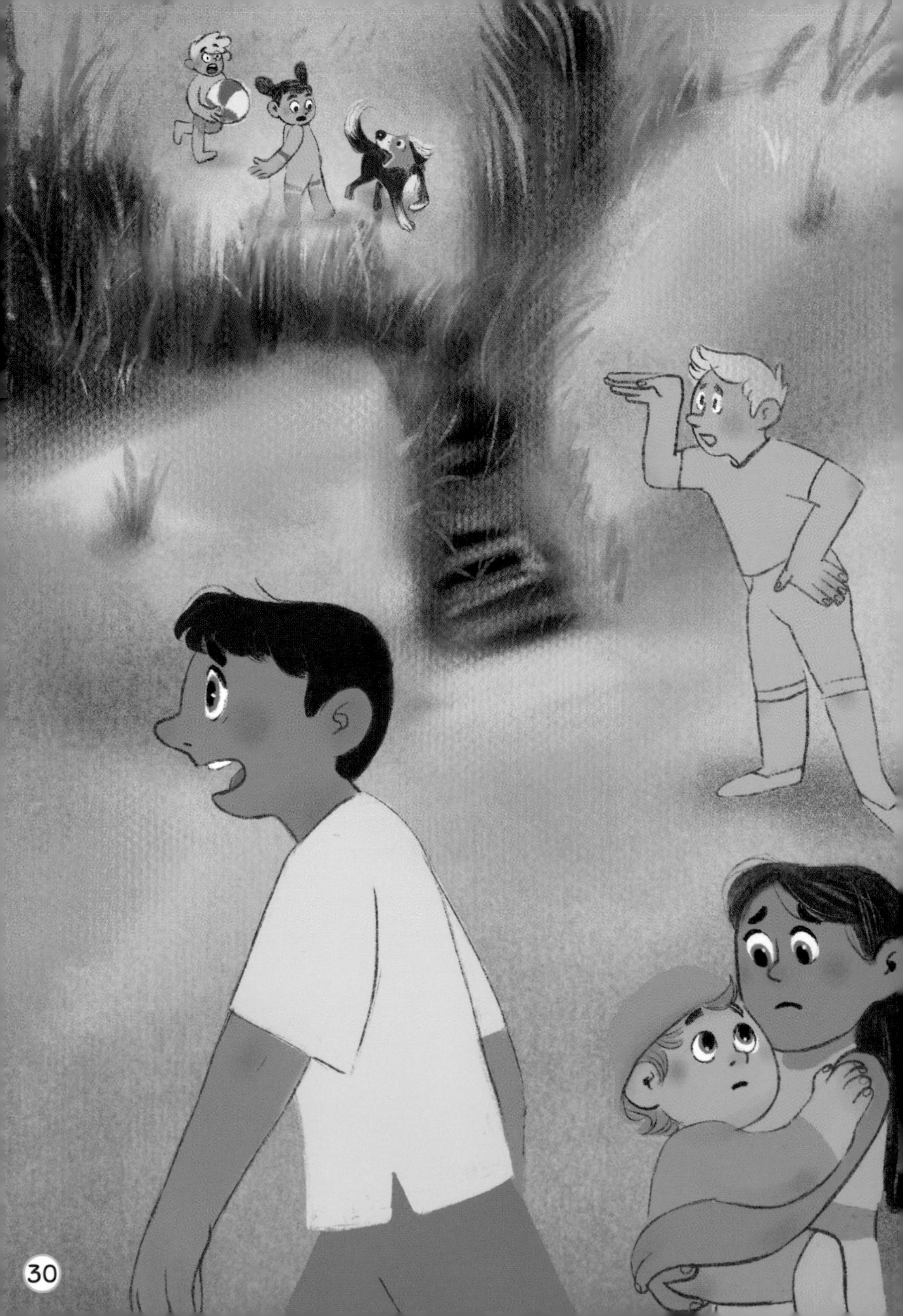

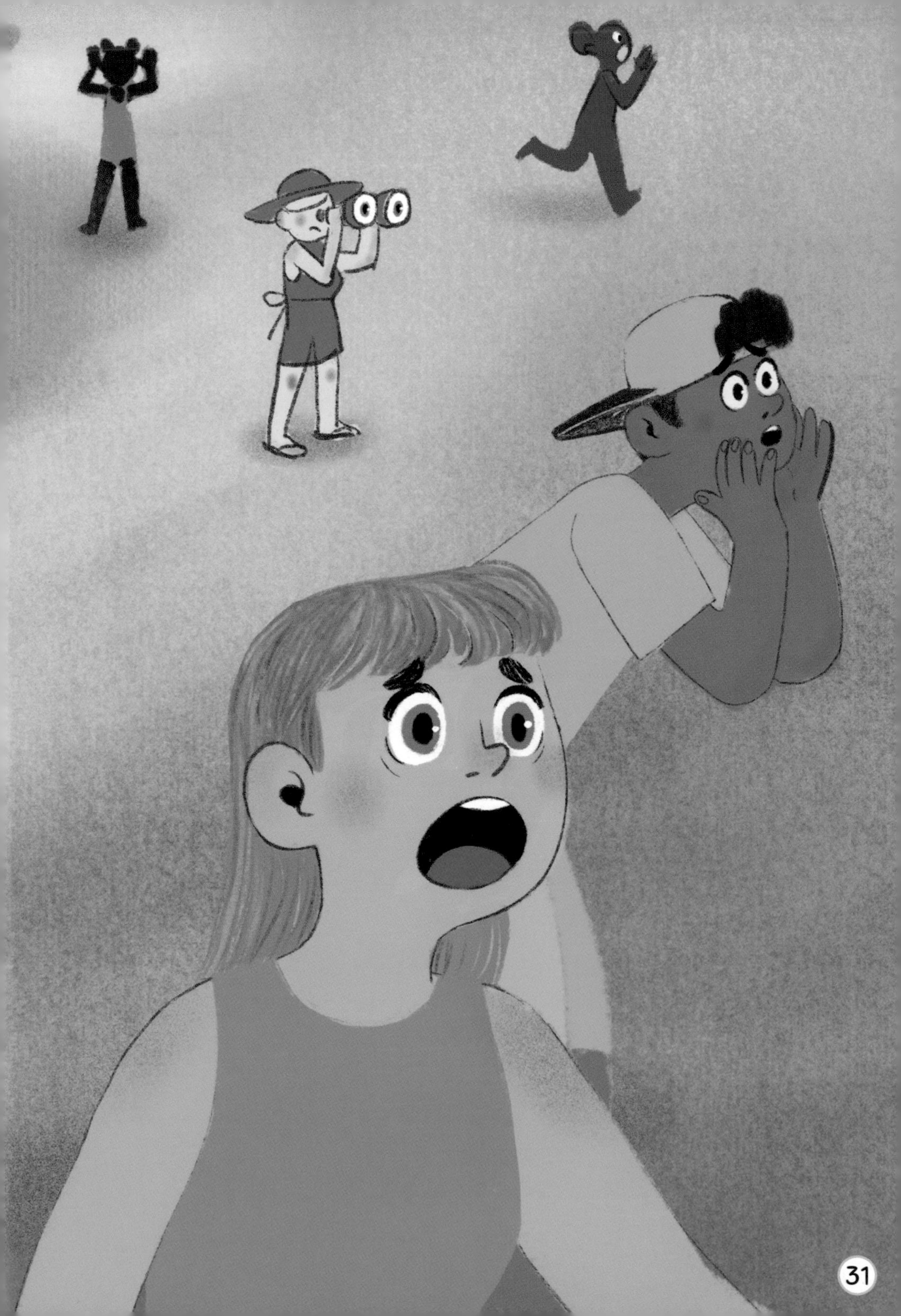

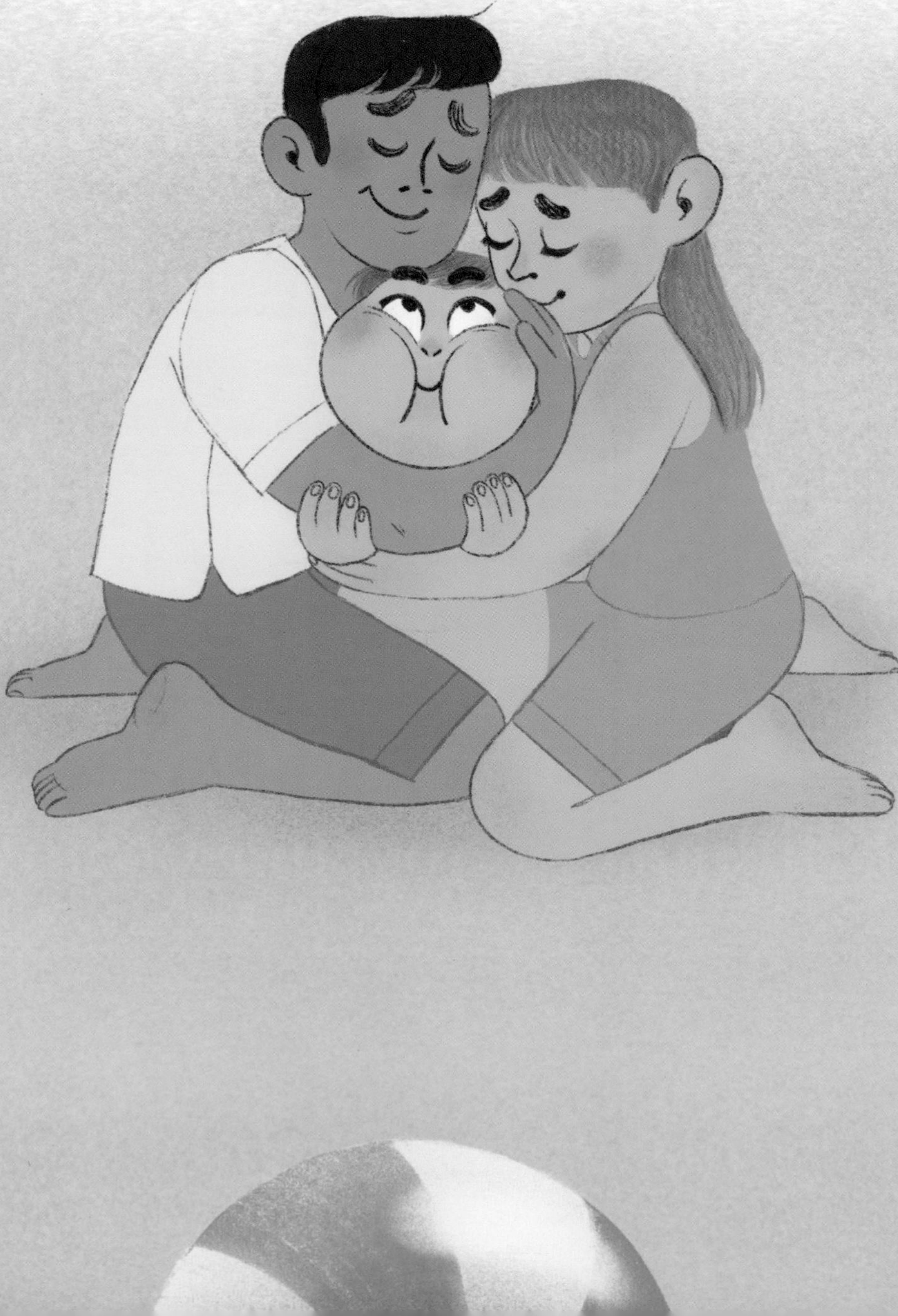